Only Opal

The Diary of a Young Girl

BY OPAL WHITELEY

SELECTED BY JANE BOULTON

ILLUSTRATIONS BY

BARBARA COONEY

PAPERSTAR

The Putnam & Grosset Group

$\mathcal{M}$y mother and father are gone.
The man did say they went to Heaven
and do live with God,
but it is lonesome without them.

The mama where I live says I am a nuisance.
I think it is something grownups
don't like to have around.
She sends me out to bring wood in.
Some days there is cream to be shaked into butter.
Some days I sweep the floor.
The mama has likes to have her house
nice and clean.

Near the road grow many flowers.
I nod to them as I go by.
They talk in shadows.
And this I have learned:
Grownups do not know the language of shadows.
Angel Mother and Angel Father did know
and they taught me.
I think sometimes Kind God
just opens the gates of Heaven
and lets them come out
to be Guardian Angels for a while.

Sometimes I read the books
that Angel Mother and Angel Father wrote in.
They tell me about all the great people.
Now I know what to name my favorite mouse.
He is Felix Mendelssohn.

I did not go to school today
for this was wash day
and the mama needed me at home.
The mama says that is my work,
but it takes a long time—
and all the time it is taking
I have longings to go explores.

My dog, Brave Horatius, came walking by.
He made a stop at the doorstop.
He wagged his tail.
That means he wants to go explores.

My crow, Lars Porsena,
flew down from the oak tree.
He landed on the back of Brave Horatius
and gave two caws.
They are friends.

All my work is done.

I am sitting on the front steps making prints.

Under the steps live some mice.

They have such beautiful eyes.

I give them bread to eat.

This morning Lars Porsena
did walk on the clean tablecloth.
He was tracking crow tracks
in jam all over it.
The mama picked me up.
And right away she did spank me
for his doing it.
I had to scrub little rubs
a long time to get it clean.

When I feel sad inside
I talk things over with my tree.
I call him Michael Raphael.
It is such a comfort
to nestle up to Michael Raphael.
He is a grand tree.
He has an understanding soul.

One day a week the mama does send me
to take eggs to all the folks hereabouts.
Today is taking egg day.
I put on my blue bonnet.
I put Felix Mendelssohn in my pocket.
He likes to go for walks.
And sometimes he sleeps in my sleeve.
Felix Mendelssohn has likes for cheese.

New folks live by the mill.
Dear Love her young husband does call her.
They are so happy.
When I gave her the eggs she smiled glad smiles
and kissed me — two on the cheeks
and one on the nose.
Then I had glad feels all over,
and Felix Mendelssohn poked his nose
out of my sleeve.
She gave him a pat
and I knew Dear Love was my friend.

One way the road does go
to the house of the girl who has no seeing.
She likes to touch the flowers I bring her.
She has seeing by feeling.
I tell her cloud ships are sailing
over the hills in a hurry.
She shuts her eyes when I shut mine.
We ride in a cloud — a fleecy white one.

I came to the house of Dear Love.
Dear Love was so glad to see me.
She was cutting out flannel patches for a quilt.
She thought one patch would be
a nice blanket for Felix Mendelssohn.
He is a soft mouse that likes soft feels
to go to sleep in.
She marked his initials on it with red ink.
F. M. on the corner.

At night the wind goes walking in the field,
talking to the earth voices there.
I did follow her down potato rows,
and her goings made ripples on my nightgown.
While I was listening to the voices of the night

Brave Horatius did catch the corner
of my nightgown in his mouth
and did pull in a most hard way
to go back to the house we live in.
He barks when he thinks it is going-home-time.

The calf is Elizabeth Barrett Browning.
I think she will be a lovely cow.
There are lonesome feels in her mooings
when her mother is away.
I put my arm around her neck.
It is such a comfort to have a friend near
when lonesome feels do come.
I took off my sunbonnet and tied it on her
so the sun wouldn't bother her eyes.
When I came home the mama did spank me real hard
and told me to go and find my sunbonnet,
and not to come back until I did find it.
I wanted to talk to Michael Raphael.

My dear pig followed me to school today.
School was already took up.
I went in first.
The new teacher told me I was tardy again.
Peter Paul Rubens walked right in.
The grunts he gave were such nice ones.
He stood there saying:
"I have come to your school.
What class are you going to put me in?"
They were the same words
I did say on my first day of school.
I guess our teacher doesn't have
understanding of pig talk.
She came at him in a hurry with a stick.

Some day I will write about Michael Raphael,
the great tree I love.
Today I did watch
and I did hear its moans
as the saw went through it.
There was a queer feel in my throat
and I couldn't stand up.
The saw did stop.
There was a stillness.
There was a queer, sad sound.
The big tree did quiver.
It did sway.
It crashed to earth.
Oh, Michael Raphael!

I am sitting on the steps for the last time.
Tomorrow we will move to a mill town.

Elizabeth Barrett Browning has been sold
with her mother, the gentle Jersey cow.

Dear Love and her husband
say Felix Mendelssohn can live
under their front steps.
They will take care of my garden.

I have walked past the house
of the girl who has no seeing.
She was not at home.

When I came for the last time
to the house of Dear Love
she was sitting on the steps
drying her hair in the sun.
It waved little ripples of light.

"I have come to say goodbye," I told her.
Dear Love smiled a sorry smile and said,
"We will never forget you."
Then she gave me a kiss on each cheek
and one on the nose.
I was so glad for the one on the nose.

I am going far away,
but Angel Mother and Angel Father
will be with me.
Guardian Angels always know
where to find you.

A NOTE ABOUT THIS BOOK

"This is a diary of my fifth and sixth year." — Opal Whiteley

It is hard to believe that someone this young could be so earnest about keeping a diary. Opal was just learning to print. Her large, crude letters were written on the backs of envelopes given to her by a kindly neighbor woman. Colored pencils came from "the fairies."

Born about 1900, according to Opal she was just five when she went to live with an Oregon family after her own parents "went to Heaven." Over the years the family lived in nineteen different lumber camps, and during that time Opal kept a diary. Even though she hid it in a secret place, under an old log, her stepsister found the diary and tore it into a million pieces. Opal saved the precious scraps in a box.

When she was twenty, Opal met a book publisher, who asked to see her diary. Opal spent nine months pasting together all the little scraps of paper. It was like doing a giant puzzle, matching up the red and green and blue words. The publisher liked her stories so much that he published them in a book.

And now you may want to start a diary of your own.

Printed on recycled paper

Text copyright © 1994 by Jane Boulton. Illustration copyright © 1994 by Barbara Cooney
All rights reserved. This book, or parts thereof, may not be reproduced in any form without permission in writing
from the publisher. A PaperStar Book, published in 1997 by The Putnam & Grosset Group, 200 Madison Avenue,
New York, NY 10016. PaperStar is a registered trademark of The Putnam Berkley Group, Inc. The PaperStar logo is
a trademark of The Putnam Berkley Group, Inc. Originally published in 1994 by Philomel Books. Opal Whiteley's
diary was first published in 1920 by The Atlantic Monthly Press and is available in a longer form, *Opal: The
Journal of an Understanding Heart,* published by Tioga Publishing Company, adapted by Jane Boulton.
Published simultaneously in Canada. Printed in the United States of America.
Library of Congress Cataloging-in-Publication Data
Boulton, Jane. Only Opal: the diary of a young girl/by Jane Boulton: illustrated by Barbara Cooney.   p.   cm.
Adaptation of: Opal, the journey of an understanding heart. Summary: A lyrical adaptation of the writings of
Opal Whiteley, in which she describes her love of nature and her life in an Oregon lumber camp at the turn of
the century. [1. Whiteley, Opal Stanley—Juvenile poetry.   2. Frontier and pioneer life—Oregon—Juvenile
poetry.   3. Oregon—Social life and customs—Juvenile poetry   4. Children's poetry.   5. Nature—Juvenile poetry.
[1. Whiteley, Opal Stanley.   2. Frontier and pioneer life—Biography.]   I. Cooney, Barbara, 1917–   ill.   II. Title
PR 9199.3.B62055   1993   813–dc20.   91-38581   CIP   AC
ISBN 0-698-11564-3
3   5   7   9   10   8   6   4   2